Vera's Talent

Doggie Tails Series

D1548680

Vera's Talent

Doggie Tails Series

By David M. Sargent, Jr.

Illustrated by Jeane Lirley Huff

Ozark Publishing, Inc.
P.O. Box 228
Prairie Grove, AR 72753

Cataloging-in-Publication Data

Sargent, David M., 1966–
    Vera's talent / by David M. Sargent, Jr. ;
illustrated by Jeane Lirley Huff.—Prairie
Grove, AR : Ozark Publishing, c2004.
    p. cm. (Doggie tails series)

    SUMMARY: Vera proves she is good for
only one thing.
    ISBN 1-56763-857-0 (hc)
    ISBN 1-56763-858-9 (pbk)

    [1. Eating—Fiction. 2. Dogs—Fiction.
3. Stories in rhyme.] I. Huff, Jeane Lirley,
1946– ill. II. Title. III. Series.

    PZ8.3.S2355Au 2004
    [E]—dc21   2003102877

Copyright © 2004 by David M. Sargent, Jr.
All rights reserved

Printed in the United States of America

iv

Inspired by

Vera's constant hunger.

Dedicated to

Those who struggle with hungry dachshunds.

Vera is smart, pretty, and fun.
But when it comes to talent,
She has only one.

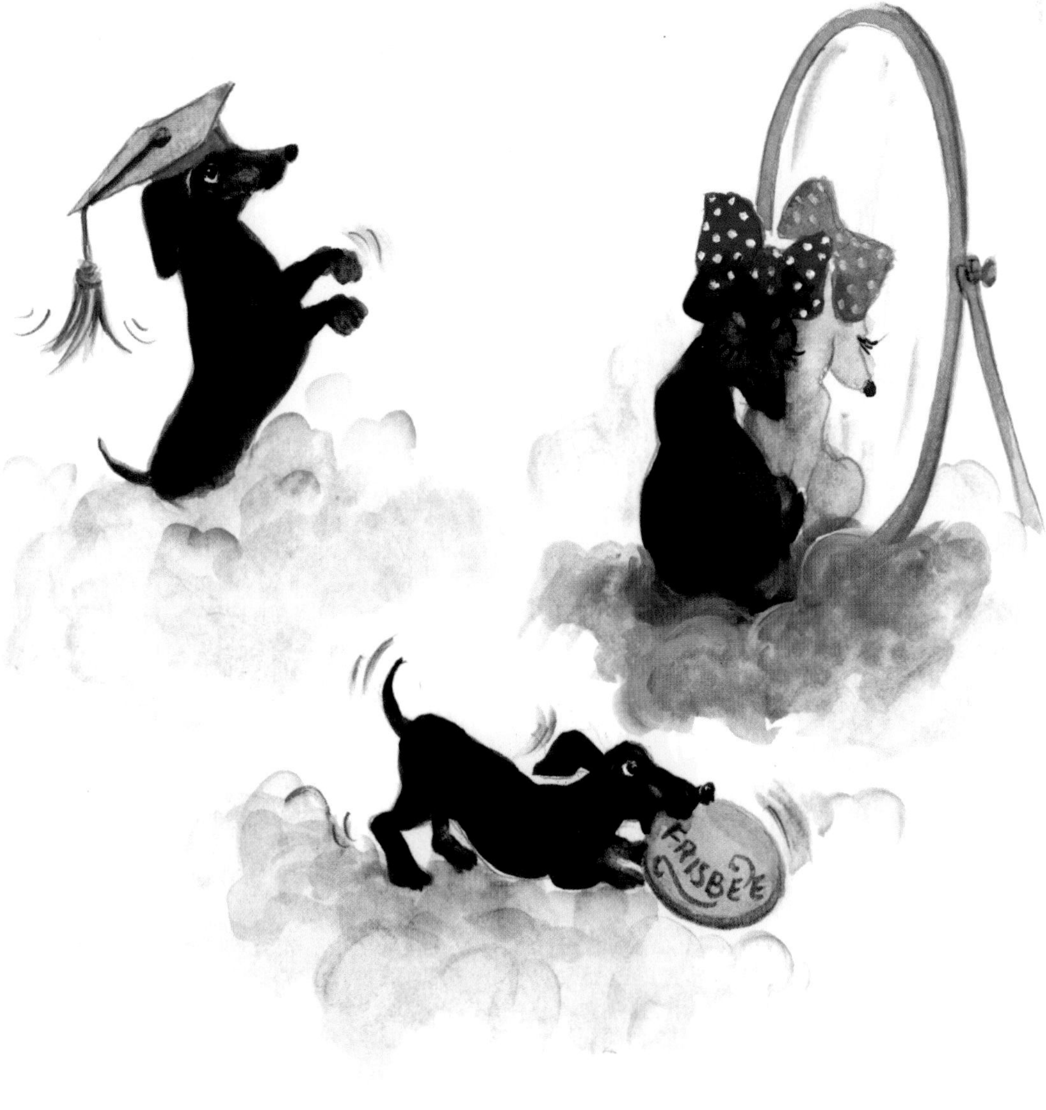
FRISBEE

It's not snorting,
Or chewing a bone.
It's not even talking
On the phone.

Her talent is one
We all possess.
But Vera's the one
Who does it best.

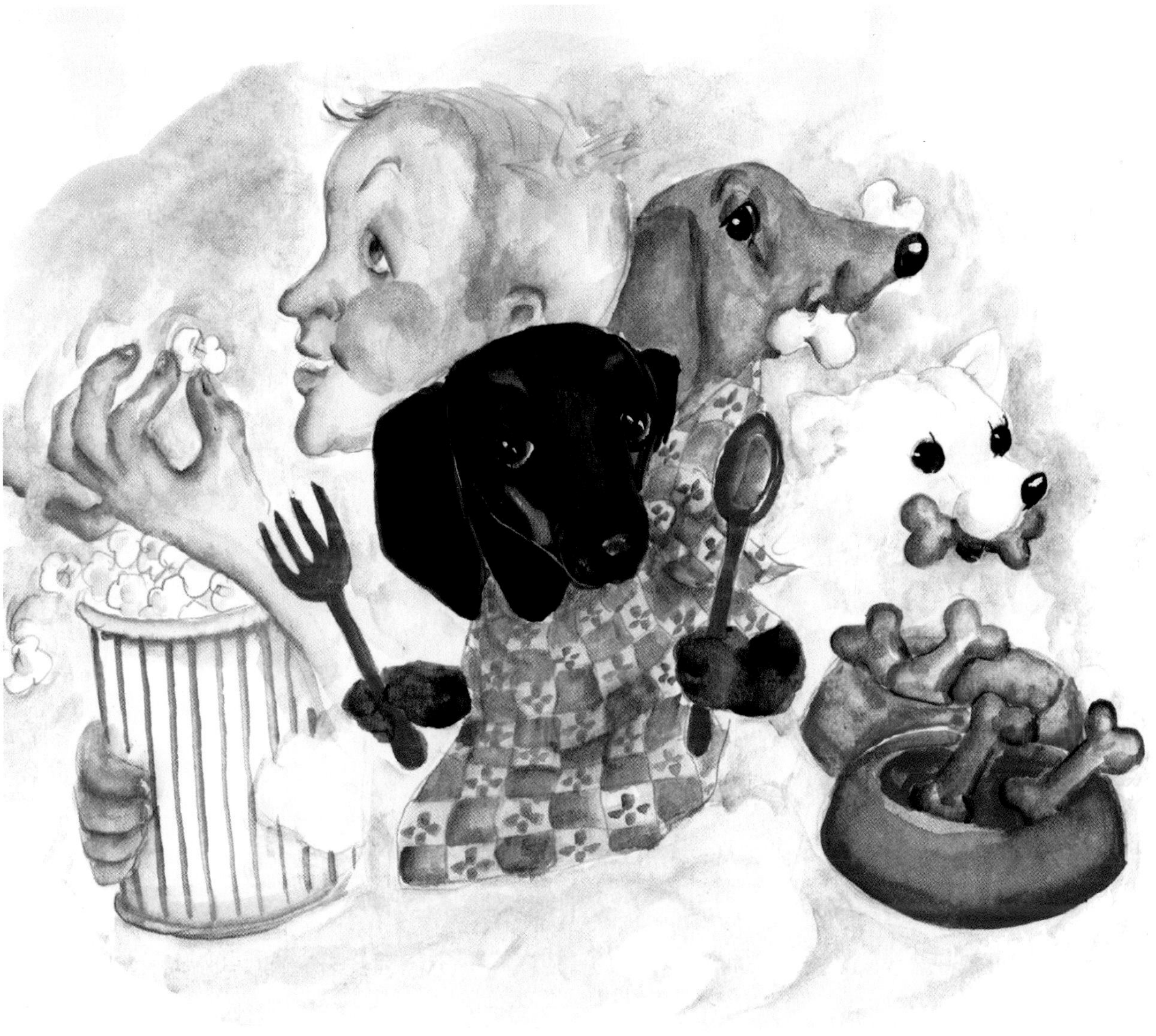

She can eat
Both day and night.
The amount she can eat
Is really a fright.

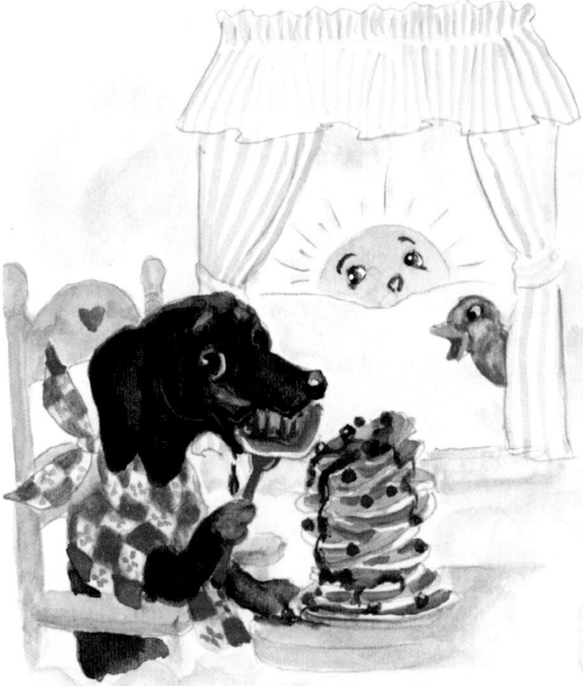

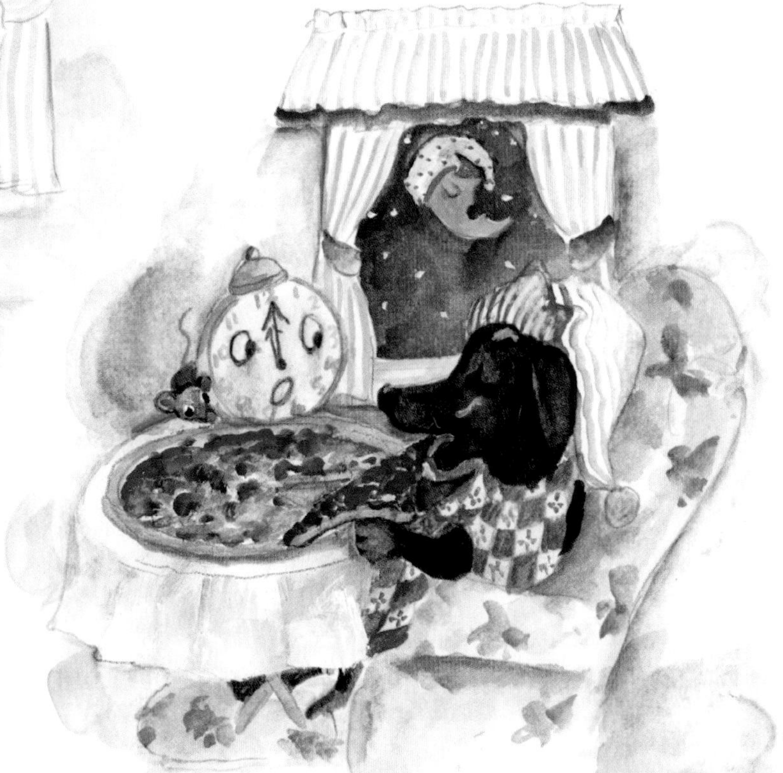

I've never seen Vera
Eat her fair share.
In fact, she's even eaten
Buffy's hair!

She's not really picky
When it comes to food.
She's quite a little pig
And sometimes rude.

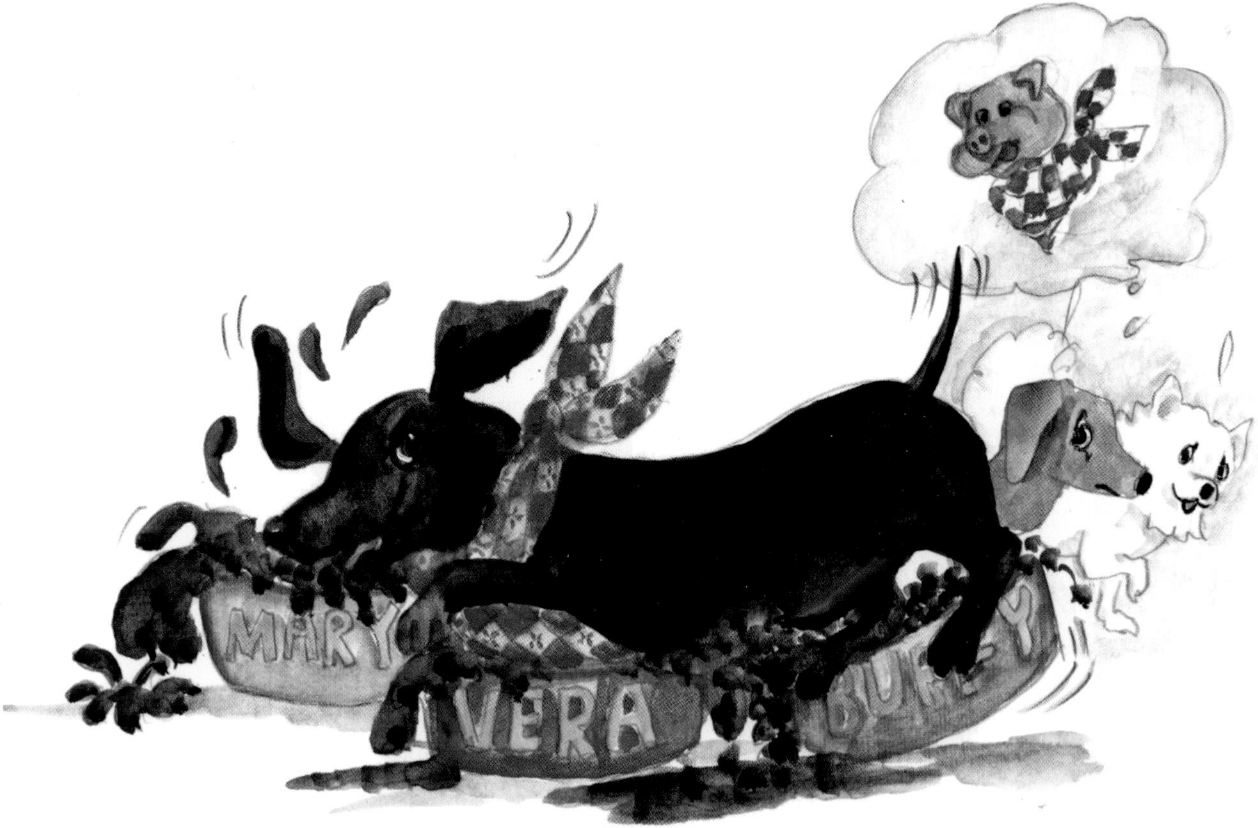
MARY
VERA

I've seen her eat
A five-pound roast.
The strange part is,
She ate it on toast!

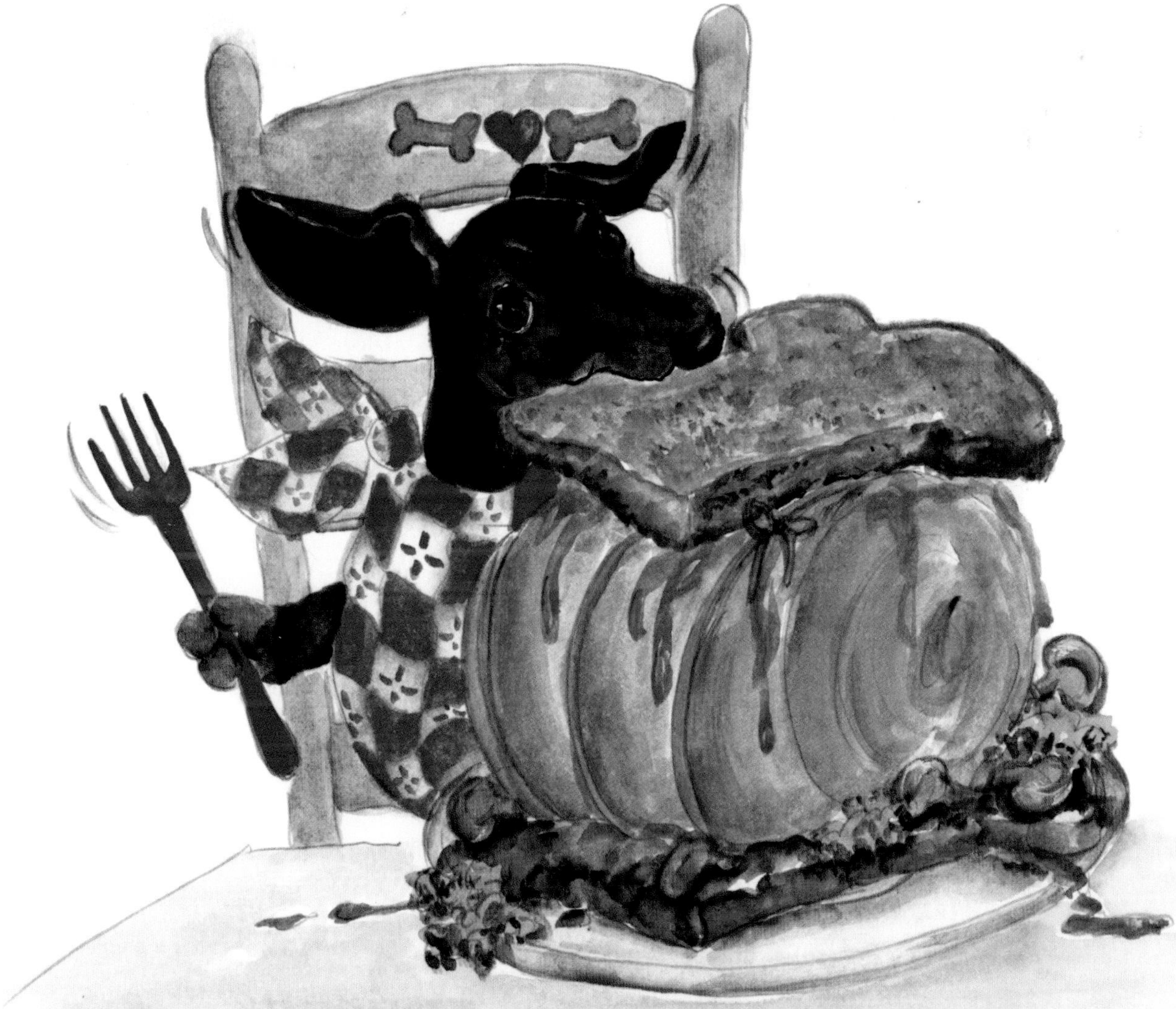

She has eaten collars,
Toys and balls.
One she really likes
Is fuzzy little dolls.

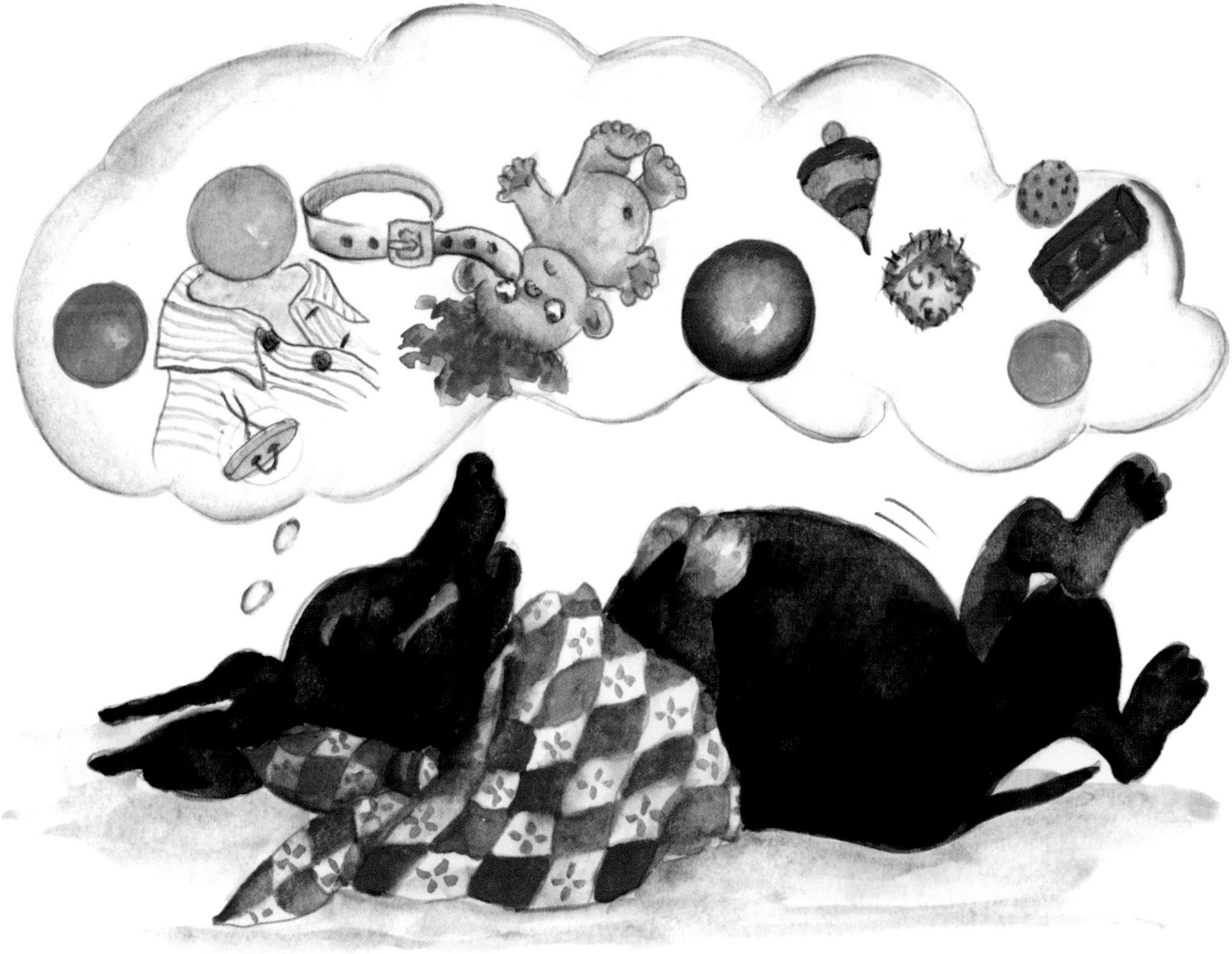

Weighing only twelve pounds,
You'd never guess,
Vera can eat
An entire turkey breast!

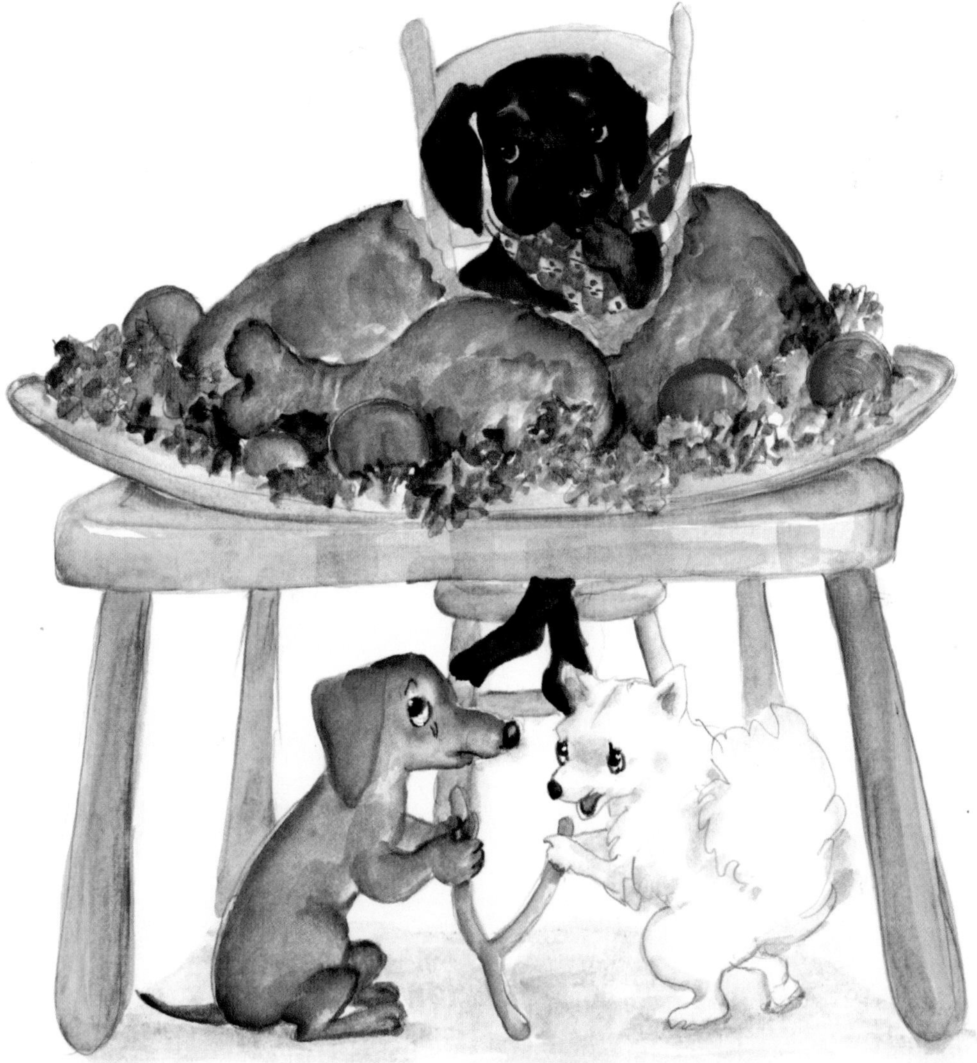

It doesn't matter
What's for lunch,
Because Vera's always
Ready to munch.

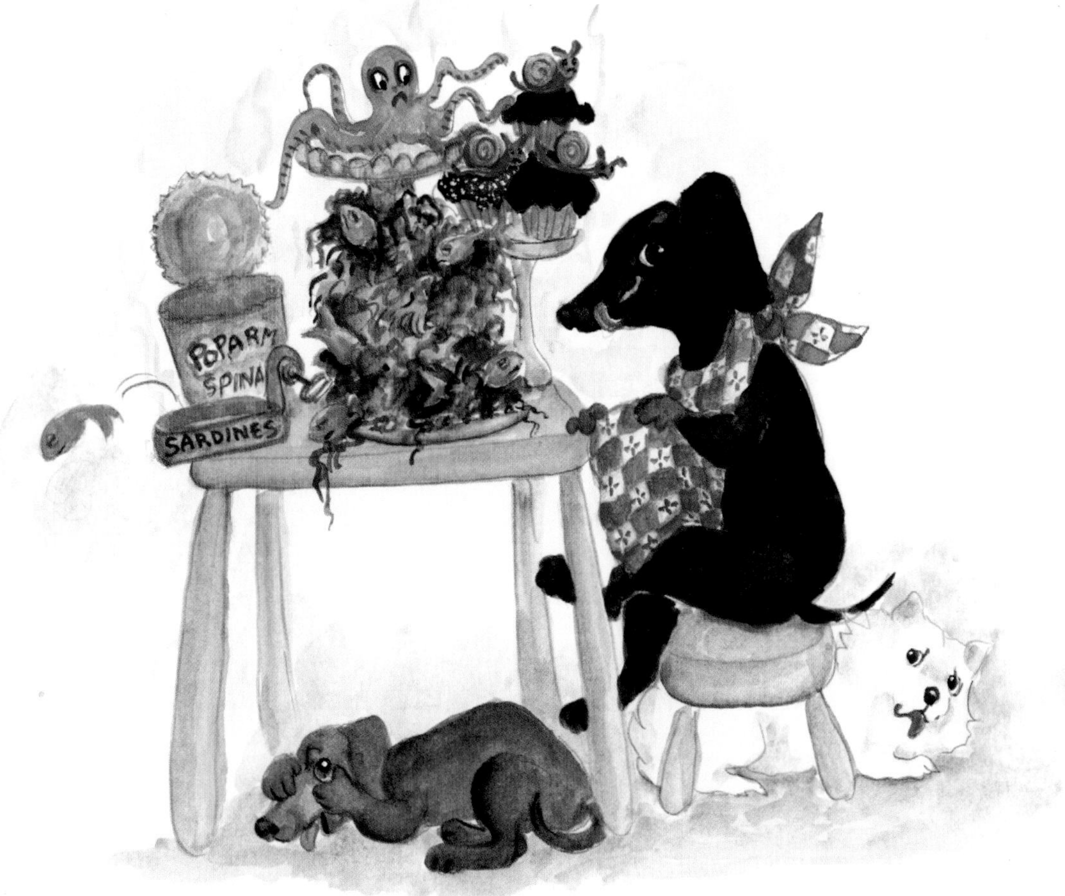
POPARM
SPINA
SARDINES

But her most favorite food,
That makes her gleam,
Is a great big scoop
Of vanilla ice cream.

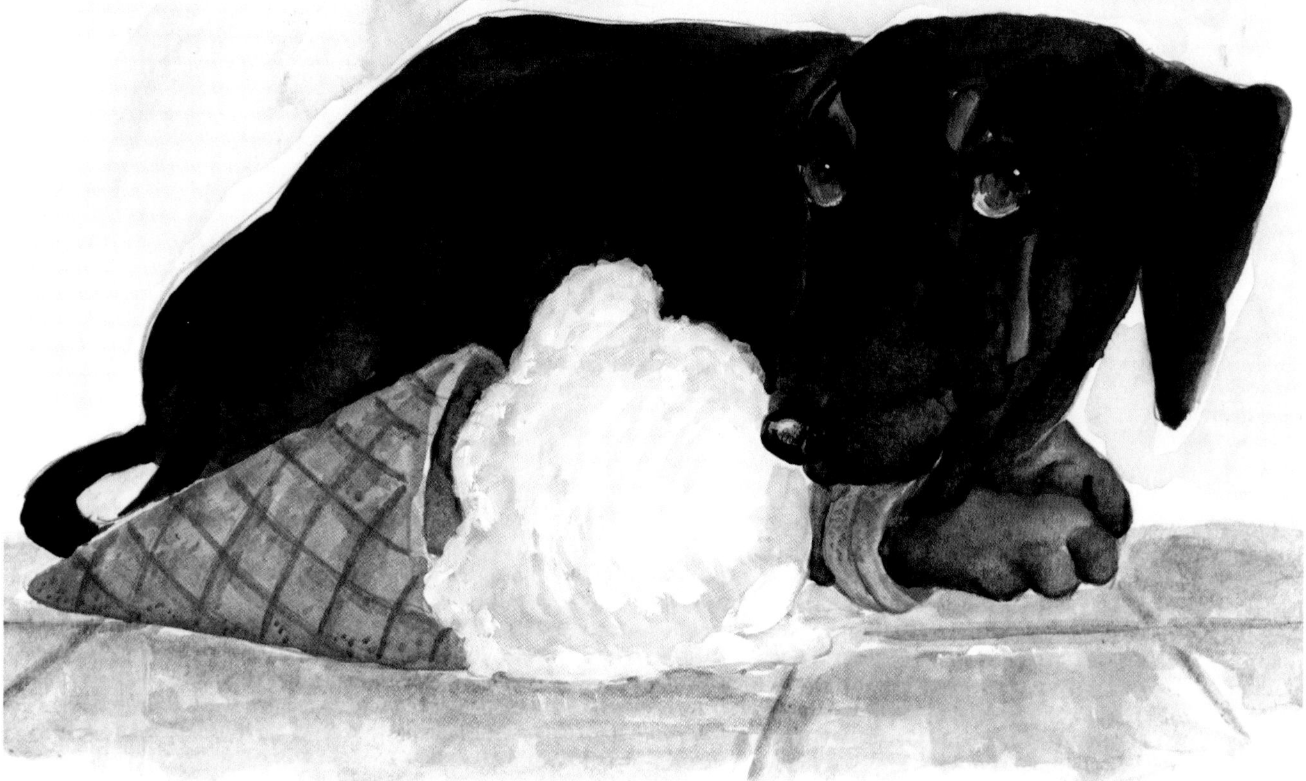

Vera's diet
Has a very wide range,
And is sometimes considered
Somewhat strange.

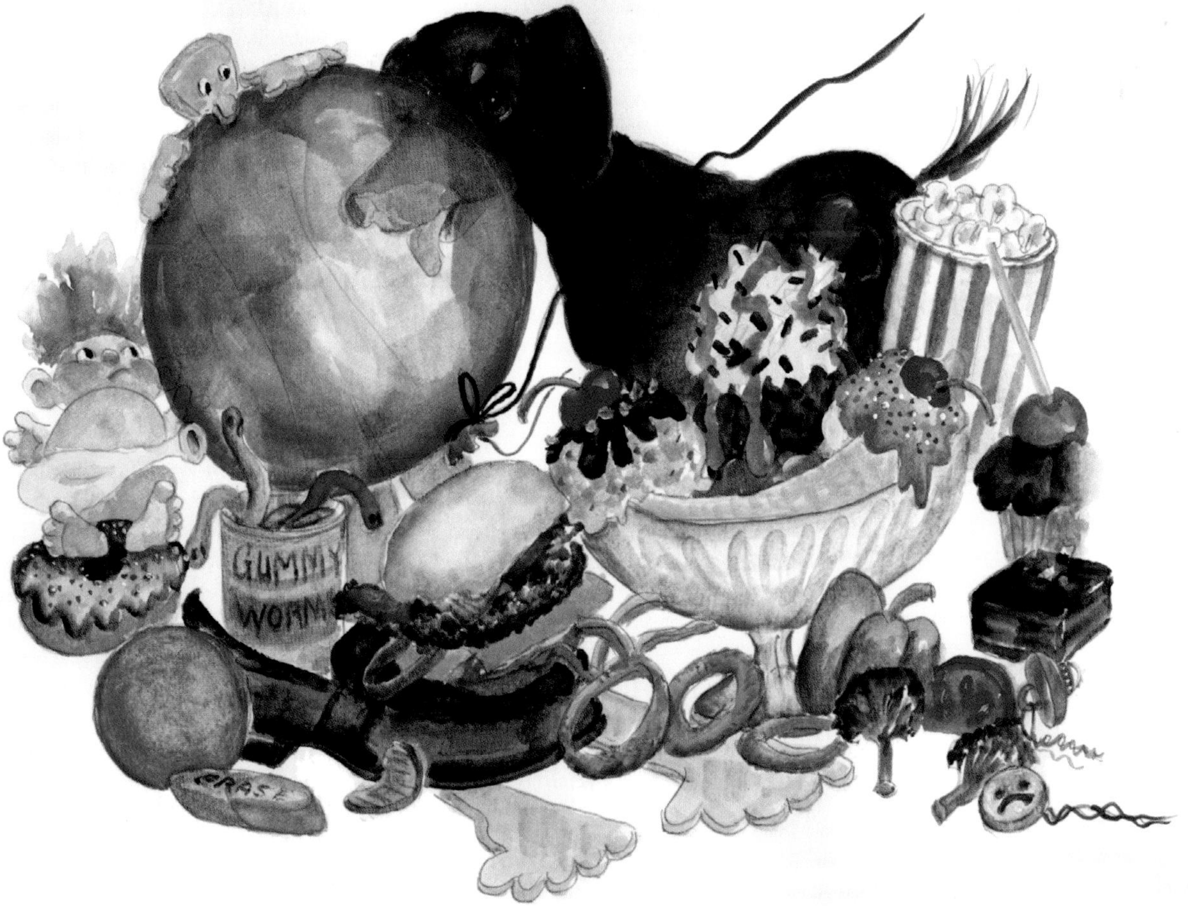
GUMMY WORMS
ERASE

As you can see,
She eats really well.
And she's never once missed
The dinner bell.

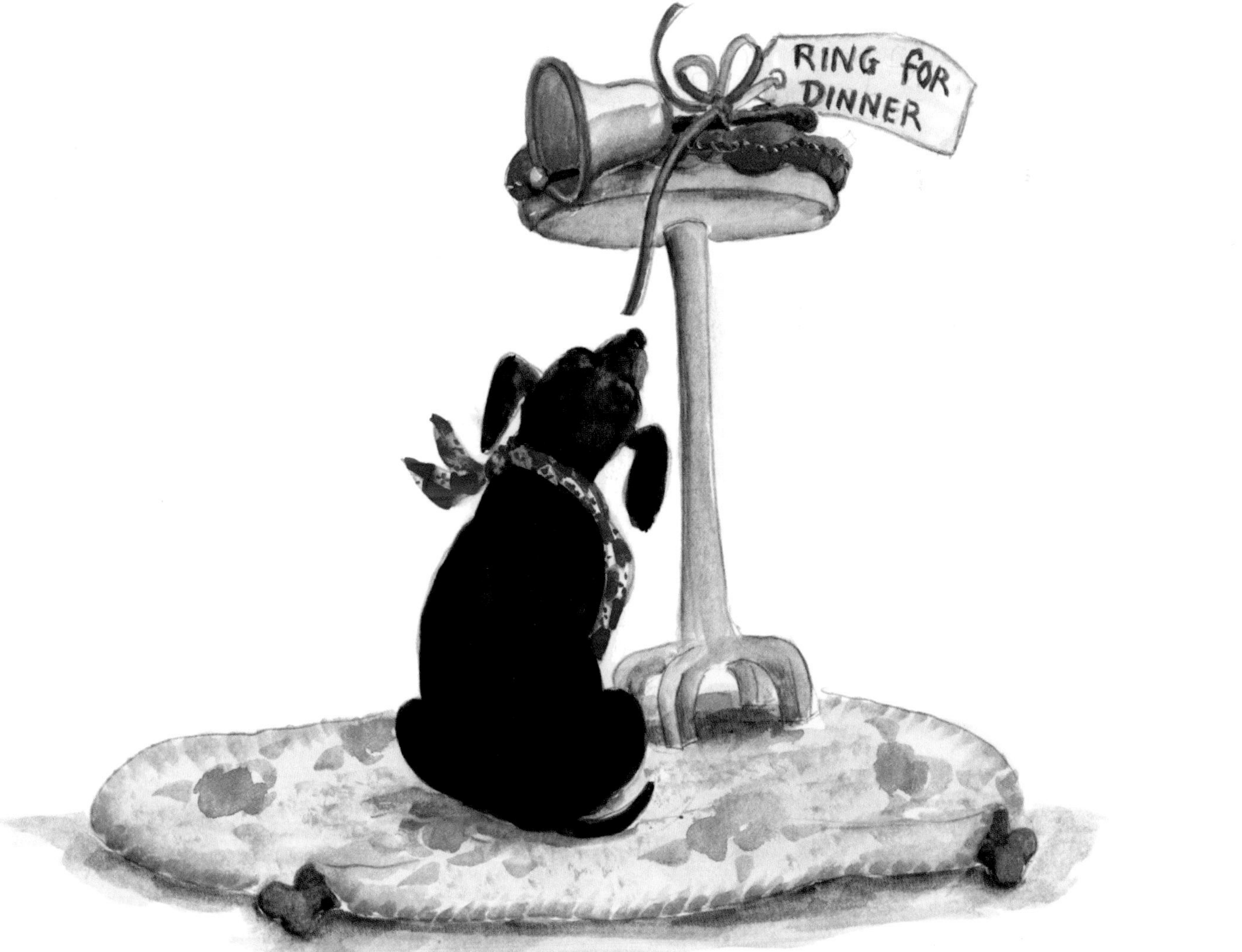
RING FOR
DINNER